JEANNE M. LEE

SILENT LOTUS

FARRAR, STRAUS & GIROUX ◄ NEW YORK

Long ago in Kampuchea, a man and a woman lived on the edge of a lake. A daughter was born to them. She was beautiful, with a face as round as the moon and eyes as bright as the stars.

The father and mother named her Lotus, like the blossoms which covered the lake. They were very happy with their baby, for she was as good as she was lovely.

Years went by, but Lotus was as silent as on the day she was born. When she was sad tears would fall from her eyes, and when she was happy smiles would light her face.

Her father and mother knew that Lotus could not hear. She could not learn to speak. They prayed to the gods, hoping they would take this misfortune away, and cherished their daughter even more.

One day, the mother and father pointed to the blossoms on the lake and to Lotus. Then the mother put her palms together with her fingers bent, forming a flower. Lotus understood. She copied her mother's gesture and so learned to name herself with her hands.

Lotus grew lovelier each day. She liked to weave baskets out of the tall grasses which grew around the lake and to swim with the turtles while her father fished. But Lotus was happiest when she walked among the herons, cranes, and white egrets, joining them in their graceful steps.

Yet Lotus would often sit by herself, lonely and sad. She wanted so much to play with the other children. But if she motioned to them, they pretended not to see. If she pulled their arms to get their attention, they ran away.

Her father and mother saw her unhappiness, but they did not know how to help her. They hoped for a sign from the gods.

Finally, they decided to go to the temple in the city. The mother put wild rice and lotus flowers in a basket as offerings; the father carried his precious daughter on his shoulders. They walked through many fields and villages, and over many canals.

When they reached the city, they hurried to the temple. Inside, the father and mother heard drums and cymbals. Lotus felt the vibrations. Then two lines of dancers appeared.

Elbows high and knees bent, Lotus imitated their movements. Long after the dancers had gone, the little girl danced. Her father and mother looked at each other. It was the sign they had hoped for.

They went to the palace. There, the queen noticed the lovely little girl and whispered to the king.

"Speak," the king said, pointing to Lotus.

"Our daughter does not speak or hear," her father said. "But she would learn to dance."

The mother motioned to her young daughter. Lotus began to dance the way she knew best, like the herons, cranes, and white egrets. The king and queen watched with delight.

"She is a most beautiful child," said the queen.

"She will learn to dance," said the king.

In the dance pavilion on the palace grounds, a graceful old woman taught Lotus how to dance the tales of the gods and kings.

Patiently, she guided the young dancer, showing her the movements that would tell those tales. Lotus learned to curl her fingers backwards and to bend her elbows and knees.

As time passed, silent Lotus began to speak with her hands, body, and feet. She loved to dance the tales of the gods and kings. And as she grew, the movements became as natural for her as the dances of the birds.

Lotus made many friends. She was no longer lonely and sad.

Finally, she was ready to dance for the king again. The court ladies dressed her in the brightest silks. They adorned her hair with gold and jasmine flowers. On her neck, arms, wrists, and ankles they put bands of precious stones and pearls.

It was the first night of the new year. Lotus danced better than she ever had, and as she danced, she saw pleasure and delight in the eyes of the people.

It was said that Lotus became the most famous dancer in the Khmer kingdom, dancing in the king's court and in the temples of the gods.

To my father